Blushing Becky

Written by
Jillian Powell

Illustrated by
Kate Sheppard

W
FRANKLIN WATTS
LONDON•SYDNEY

Jillian Powell

"We all blush sometimes. It's as natural as laughter or tears. The Ancient Greeks even had a special word for 'fear of going red'!"

Kate Sheppard

"I was always blushing, just like Becky. The more I worried about it, the more I blushed. I still blush now, but I don't mind so much!"

Becky blushed at the smallest thing.

She blushed when she sat next
to the boy she liked best in class.

She blushed even more
when he smiled at her.

Now Becky had something else to
blush about. Her class was putting
on a play at the end of term.

Becky had to paint a tree. But green
paint kept splashing EVERYWHERE!
The more green paint she splashed,
the redder she blushed.

11

The next day, it was time to learn
the words. Everyone had to stand
on stage and read aloud.

Soon it was Becky's turn.

She blushed as red as her socks.

The next week, they had to practise the music. Becky tried to play a recorder.

But it just made a horrid
squeaky sound. She blushed
as red as her jumper.

"Never mind, Becky," said her
teacher. "Try these cymbals instead."

"This is fun!" Becky thought.

Then CRASH! BANG! "Whoops!"
Becky blushed even more.

CRASH!
BANG!

19

The week after, they had to learn a dance. When the teacher stopped the music, they all had to make animal statues. Becky was being a tiger.

plink
plink
plink

Becky stopped ...

... she wobbled ...

... then she fell over.

And Becky blushed as red
as her hair ribbons.

Now it was time to make the
costumes. They needed animal
masks for the dance. Becky
made a fierce tiger mask.

25

At last, everything was ready. It was
time for everyone to come and watch.

27

snap snap

"Well done!" they all cheered
and clapped when it was over.

And Becky blushed redder
than ever ...

30

... but Tiger didn't!

Notes for parents and teachers

READING CORNER has been structured to provide maximum support for new readers. The stories may be used by adults for sharing with young children. Primarily, however, the stories are designed for newly independent readers, whether they are reading these books in bed at night, or in the reading corner at school or in the library.

Starting to read alone can be a daunting prospect. READING CORNER helps by providing visual support and repeating words and phrases, while making reading enjoyable. These books will develop confidence in the new reader, and encourage a love of reading that will last a lifetime!

If you are reading this book with a child, here are a few tips:

1. Make reading fun! Choose a time to read when you and the child are relaxed and have time to share the story.

2. Encourage children to reread the story, and to retell the story in their own words, using the illustrations to remind them what has happened.

3. Give praise! Remember that small mistakes need not always be corrected.

READING CORNER covers three grades of early reading ability, with three levels at each grade. Each level has a certain number of words per story, indicated by the number of bars on the spine of the book, to allow you to choose the right book for a young reader:

GRADE 1	GRADE 2	GRADE 3
50 words	130 words	250 words
70 words	160 words	350 words
100 words	200 words	450 words